Puppy Mudge
Has a Snack

By Cynthia Rylant

Illustrated by Isidre Mones

in the style of Suçie Stevenson

SCHOLASTIC INC.

New York   Toronto   London   Auckland   Sydney
Mexico City   New Delhi   Hong Kong   Buenos Aires

ISBN 0-439-56135-3

Text copyright © 2003 by Cynthia Rylant. Illustrations copyright © 2003 by Suçie Stevenson. All rights reserved. Published by Scholastic Inc., 557 Broadway, New York, NY 10012, by arrangement with Simon & Schuster Books for Young Readers, Simon & Schuster Children's Publishing Division. SCHOLASTIC and associated logos are trademarks and/or registered trademarks of Scholastic Inc.

12 11 10 9 8 7 6 5 4 3   4 5 6 7 8 9/0

Printed in the U.S.A.   23

First Scholastic printing, January 2004

Book design by Mark Siegel
The text of this book is set in Goudy.
The illustrations are rendered in pen-and-ink and watercolor.

This is Mudge.

He is Henry's puppy.

Mudge wants Henry's snack.

"No, Mudge," says Henry.

Mudge gets on Henry's lap.

"No, Mudge," says Henry.

Mudge wants Henry's snack.

Mudge gets on Henry's head.

"No, Mudge," says Henry.

Mudge wants Henry's snack.

Mudge drools.

Mudge looks cute.

Mudge looks very, very cute.

Mudge looks too cute.

"Mudge, you are TOO cute,"
says Henry.

Henry gets a snack for Mudge.
It is a CRACKER.

Mudge LOVES crackers.

Now Henry has a snack.
And Mudge has a snack.

And all Mudge had to be was
CUTE!